WHO FLUNG DUNG?

Written and illustrated by

Ben Redlich

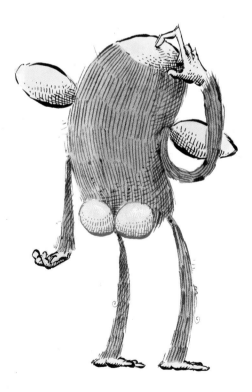

little bee

FOR
MY NIECE & NEPHEW,
RACHEL MAY
&
CARL BRANDON REDLICH,
B.R.

First published in 2006
by Meadowside Children's Books
185 Fleet Street
London EC4A 2HS

This edition published in 2008 by Little Bee
an imprint of Meadowside Children's Books

A CIP catalogue record for this book
is available from the British Library

ISBN 13 pbk 978-1-84539-400-4

10 9 8 7 6 5 4 3 2
Printed in Malaysia

One pleasant day, Furley the monkey was minding his own business when...

SHOOP!

"Who flung dung?"
Furley said, in need of a towel.

No one was around to confess,
so he went to investigate.

After a short while, he saw Elephant and Rhinoceros.

"Who flung dung?"
Furley yelled accusingly.

"Don't look at us!" said Elephant,
"I'd sooner trample you to dust,
than do such a filthy thing!"

"And I'd sooner run at you
and prod you with my nose!"
said Rhinoceros.

"Now, be on your way!"

Furley went on his way.

He soon bumped into
Python and Crocodile.

"Who flung dung?"
Furley screeched at both of them.

"Don't be ridiculous!" said Python, "Even if I could, I wouldn't do such a sorry thing! I'd sooner squeeze you tight and swallow you whole!"

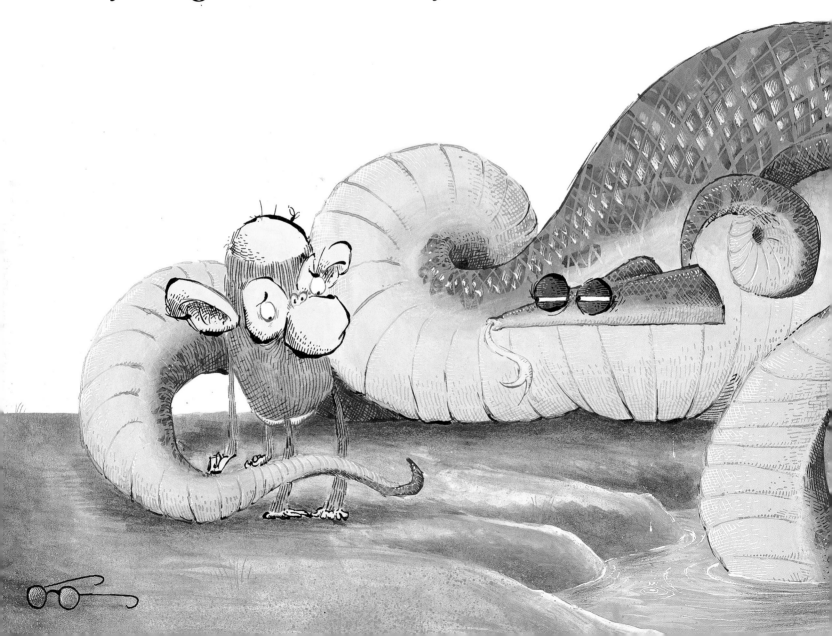

"And I'd sooner snap you up and scoff you down!" said Crocodile. "Now be on your way!"

Furley pushed on in search of the culprit...

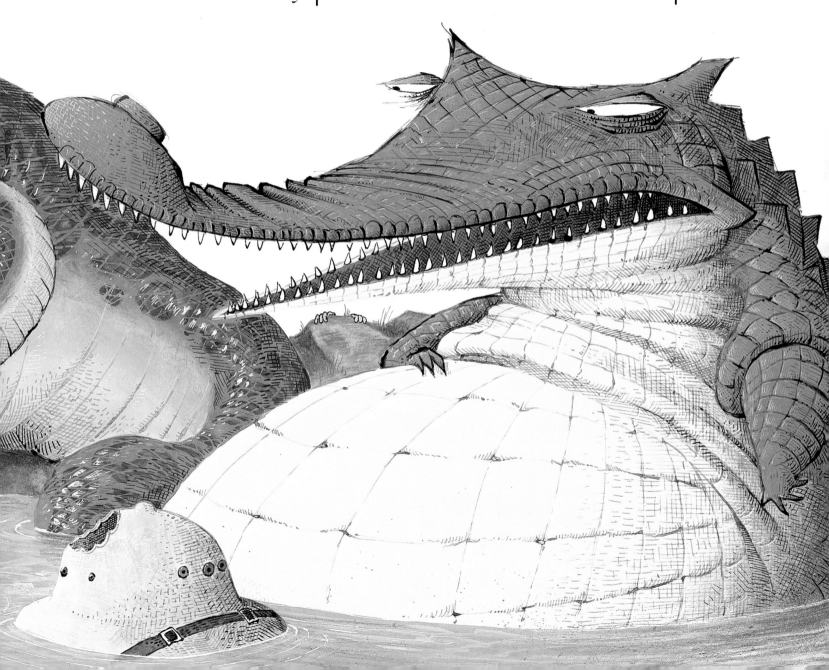

Before long he saw Lion.

"Who flung dung?" Furley demanded to know.

"Silly monkey!" said Lion. "Why I'd sooner hunt you down and gobble you up, than do such a horrid thing. Be on your way!"

Just then he saw Vulture and her friends.

"Who flung dung?"
Furley yelled
accusingly.

"Don't be vulgar!" said Vulture.
"We'd sooner pick your bones,
than do such a ghastly thing.
Be on your way!"

On Furley went...

Just then he heard something in the tree.

It sounded like giggling...

It was his brother, Charlie,
looking awfully suspicious.

"You flung dung!"

Furley bellowed knowingly.

"That's right!" said Charlie.
"And what are you going to do about it?"

SHOOP!